Words; Wreaths
Winter Collections Vol.2

Various Authors

Ukiyoto Publishing

All global publishing rights are held by

Ukiyoto Publishing

Published in 2021

Content Copyright © Ukiyoto

ISBN 9789364946773

All rights reserved.
No part of this publication may be reproduced, transmitted, or stored in a retrieval system, in any form by any means, electronic, mechanical, photocopying, recording or otherwise, without the prior permission of the publisher.

The moral rights of the author have been asserted.

This is a work of fiction. Names, characters, businesses, places, events, locales, and incidents are either the products of the author's imagination or used in a fictitious manner. Any resemblance to actual persons, living or dead, or actual events is purely coincidental.

This book is sold subject to the condition that it shall not by way of trade or otherwise, be lent, resold, hired out or otherwise circulated, without the publisher's prior consent, in any form of binding or cover other than that in which it is published.

*"Be ahead of all parting, as though it already were
behind you, like the winter that has just gone by.
For among these winters there is one so endlessly winter
that only by wintering through it will your heart survive."*

— Rainer Maria Rilke

CONTENTS

One sultry afternoon	1
A folio of feelings	12
Talk of the dead	22
Who are you	29
Eternity	32
The Ice Cream	35
The Anklet On Her Left Foot	40
Poetry Collections	52
Anjaane Rishte	63
How my life is	76
The Black Pawn	82
About the Authors	*85*

One sultry afternoon
by Akber Ayub

From the sunlit patio of their suburban home Niloufer squinted at their sun-speckled yard. The late October sunshine bathed parts of the courtyard and threw flecks of light on the paved pathway that led to the big iron gates in front. Scattered dry leaves, shrubs and flowers lent a rustic touch.

This was her favourite spot. She would often retreat here to be lulled by nature...much like a child in its mother's lap. And the white-and-grey cat that lay snoozing under the dappled shade of their gnarled old mango tree accentuated the feeling. Her mother would toss an occasional biscuit or a slice of bread to the old feline and with that patronage the cat had laid claim to the yard. She snoozed around here most of the day, especially on lazy afternoons like this.

A sudden puff of wind gusted through the foliage dislodging a bunch of dry leaves on a twig that thudded to the ground. The cat perked up its ears, opened an eye, and looked at Niloufer. Not finding her quite interesting, it went back to snoozing. The yard lay veiled in a kind of torpor; only the whispering branches broke the afternoon silence.

The courtyard held her attention for a brief while then the angst began seeping back into her mind—spreading like ink on paper.

A vein in her temples began to throb. She lingered a while longer then retreated to her bedroom upstairs. On her way up she heard her grandma snoring softly from her bedroom; and the bare feet of their live-in maid stuck out on a mat from under the stairway. An afternoon siesta formed their favourite indulgence.

From the front veranda the aging, brass-and-wood clock struck the hour: two long clangs. That was another legacy left by her late father—apart from, of course, their land: nearly hundred acres of fertile paddy fields on the outskirts of town. Ever since he passed away three years ago, their devoted staff provided all the help her mother needed. Of course, the business end of it had all been tied up very well by her father.

Niloufer slumped into the padded armchair by the window. The day was warm and sultry despite the breeze. She could hear the wind in the leaves and the steady hum of the ceiling fan that hung from wooden rafters and spun halfheartedly.

Why is he taking so long, she thought. Nishath, her only cousin, lived on the other end of town. He'd reached the hospital around noon to relieve her so she could come home for a quick lunch.

"You look so tired," he'd said.

But of course. She'd hardly slept the previous night—dozing fitfully, waking up every so often and craning her neck to look over at her mother on the other bed in the room. Reassured by the soft cadence of her breathing she would drift into another catnap, sleeping in snatches.

Now, after a hurried lunch, she'd tried to catch a few winks but sleep eluded her. A constant stream of shifting thoughts ran through her mind creating a jumble of emotions.

It had all started exactly a month ago. Initially her mother had complained of a dull ache in her lower abdomen. Then an occasional, searing pain. That's when she took her to the district hospital. Medical tests revealed…*an ovarian cyst!* Then the bleeding began, at first sporadically, then more frequently. The doctors advised—quite bluntly Niloufer thought—immediate hysterectomy: surgical removal of her uterus. The news stunned her, as though someone had plunged a knife into her. For some time, she toyed with the idea of taking a second opinion from a private hospital in the city, but the doctors were insistent that no opinion can change the verdict: an immediate surgical procedure, else, they cautioned, her life could be in danger.

And yet there was a chilling paradox: the delicate procedure itself was risky. Despite all the care and attention, they said, there was still a chance that something could go wrong. They'd try their best, they said. Niloufer left the doctor's room in a daze, overwhelmed with the crushing sense of irony. Anxiously, in the next few days, she began ferreting out information on ovarian cysts. As she probed, she discovered that hysterectomy is indeed a risky procedure and fatalities have been reported from botched procedures. The weeks that followed were a whirlwind of consultations and dealing with agonizing thoughts and emotions. Oh, how she missed her father…leaving her alone to deal with such a painful event. At times her thoughts raged like a storm…and in the eye of the storm she saw the kind, beatific face of her mother, helpless and vulnerable, caught in the whirlwind of destiny. Then, from that vortex, like a rising phoenix, a stubborn resolve grew inside her: *she'd save her mother at any cost, come what may.*

Several days had passed since then. The surgery was last Monday. Today was Thursday; so that made it three days.

Three days…that felt like three months.

It was evident that despite all their subsequent reassurances, the doctors had botched up the surgery. They wouldn't admit it, of course, but now, after three agonising days, it is becoming clear as daylight. Her mother lay in a suspended coma, surfacing intermittently from deep oblivion, her life hanging by a thread that, at times threatened to snap! Niloufer shuddered as snippets of thoughts darted through her mind and threw up murky images.

Anxious days melded into torturous nights. And the following morning, in the stillness of dawn, she heard the approaching footsteps of destiny. She tried brushing away her nagging thoughts but like an ill wind that refused to go away they remained, until she heard the eerie footfalls of fate.

As noon approached on the third day, Nishath had come to the hospital once again. All through the ordeal he had been a pillar of strength, shoring up her spirits when she felt low, spurring her on when she seemed to wilt under pressure. As soon as he'd reached his aunt's bedside, he insisted that she go home for lunch and a brief rest. She refused, but finally, despite a near sleepless night and an agonising morning, she had relented. He'd dropped her home hurriedly on his bike and then dashed back to the hospital. He had promised to keep her updated constantly, and whenever she was home, she awaited his calls and messages.

This morning while she was at the hospital a senior doctor was on his rounds. He reached her mother's bedside, looked at the charts, went through the file that the matron carried, then consulted the resident doctors briefly. To her anxious queries he had been contrite and had said little. But she gathered that her mother was responding well to treatment and that if she made it through the next 12 hours she'd recover. Oh, even though that was not the least bit reassuring, Niloufer had felt a quick wave of relief wash over her.

Now, seated in the armchair she grabbed her mobile and called Nishath, but his line was engaged. He'd promised to pick her up in an hour. She hurriedly tapped out a message to him. Then she waited as minutes ticked by.

Five minutes later there was still nothing. She checked to see if he had seen her message. He hadn't. She called his number, but once again, it was engaged. Who's he calling, she wondered. And why isn't he replying? Over the last three days it'd become something like a routine, whenever he left her home for rest. She left the armchair and went downstairs. Then she walked hurriedly toward the narrow cement staircase that led to their basement.

A thought had been spinning in her mind since morning—ever since the doctor's visit. She remembered the amulet an old priest had given them once, stashed away in a wooden chest in the basement. He had said it'd ward off all evil if you tied it to your arm. It had amazing healing powers. She'd fetch that amulet and tie it to her mother's arm. All right, she wasn't much of a believer in all this—much like her father. But her mother held an obscure faith in these mystics. It can do no harm, she decided. But if it helped, then why not? She strode toward the corner staircase in the hall and tramped down hurriedly.

Then it happened.

She missed a step, staggered, and seemed to regain her balance, but then she missed her footing and went tumbling down the steps, landing on her leg with a dull thud. The cold cement steps soaked up all sound, and her granny and the maid hardly stirred. Her mobile landed on a rolled-up rug, glanced off and slid toward a worn-out chair next to the wooden chest.

For some moments Niloufer lay still, catching her breath, and her wits around her. Then she stirred; and a pang of pain shot through her right foot.

Soft sunlight crept through the door at the head of the stairs. A puff of air blew in, disturbing fine dust on the floor that swirled up into a cloud. Motes of dust danced in the shaft of sunlight.

Lying prone on the cold floor she willed herself to get to her feet. Has she twisted her ankle, or worse, broken it? She had to rush to the hospital, she reminded herself. Once again, she tried to move her leg and winced as another spasm of pain surged through her leg.

Suddenly the pain, the agony, and the tension of the last two months rushed at her in a torrent.

Niloufer burst into tears.

Ever so slowly, she curled into a little ball. Waves of pent-up grief and helplessness washed over her as she sobbed. Her foetal form shuddered as she wept, her sighs and whines ringing softly in the still air. Oddly, held in the grip of her grief, her own plaintive wails sounded eerily like a swansong…a requiem! Almost like the poignant cry of a lost child. Quickly she shook herself out of the spell.

This is bizarre. Oh God, what's happening to me?

Gradually the sobs subsided. Then she lifted her head and looked through teary eyes at the wooden chest set against the far wall.

I'll have to retrieve that amulet.

Clenching her teeth, Niloufer inched forward. She half crawled, half dragged herself to the vault, then, gritting her teeth, hauled herself into a sitting position. She pulled at the top drawer; but it refused to budge. With a hard set to her face, she yanked at the handle with all the strength she could muster and the drawer flung open and crashed to the floor. The small, circular wooden box that carried the amulet pirouetted an arm's length away. Leaning forward she retrieved it.

Sweat beaded her forehead.

Now, she inched forward once again and retrieved her phone. After a moment she reached for the chair, pulled it to her and, gingerly, hoisted herself onto it. A soft prayer escaped her lips as she perched on the chair.

Why isn't Nishath calling? He hasn't replied to her earlier message either. Has something happened? Has her mother…*oh, stop!* Don't let your imagination run wild. But then, inexplicably, she was filled with a sudden dread. What if she called Nishath and he had some terrible news!? What if…? She won't be able to take it, she told herself. Is her worst nightmare about to come true? *God…keep my mother safe…spare her life!*

There was still no communication from him. Her mind darted toward different possibilities. She shook her head to clear it, but the thoughts wouldn't go away. As moments passed, she felt a sinking feeling prodding at her heart.

And then, just as she slumped on the chair with a sigh of resignation, her phone buzzed. She unlocked it and stared at the screen. Finally! It was his message.

But when she read it, she nearly stopped breathing. *What in God's name is this?*

'AUNTY NOT RESPONDING; SHIFTED TO ICU. VITAL SIGNS DOWN. RUSH AT ONCE.'

Niloufer sprang from the chair and hobbled toward the stairway. Pain had stopped registering; her whole body felt numb, freed from pain. Like in a trance she climbed the stairs, then limped across her slumbering home and reached the gates.

Flagging down a passing rickshaw she climbed into it and headed for the hospital. Blood rushed into her head and made a pounding sound in her ears. Her agony etched on her grim face, she thought, *I wish I could turn back the clock and bring the wheels of time to a stop.*

*

There was a buzz of activity outside the ICU. She saw Nishath and hobbled towards him, her face ashen. *"What happened?"*

"She is in there."

Her eyes bored into his face. "Is she…alright? Tell me, what did they say?"

"Shshsh…" A matronly nurse gestured to her, finger on her lips.

Nishath touched her shoulder tenderly. She looked at him deadpan, all emotions drained from her face. "Is anything…wrong?" she whispered with a quiver in her voice.

Nishath gulped. He didn't reply immediately.

Niloufer held him in a fixed gaze as though to anchor herself to sanity. An eerie feeling gripped her now…as if her world was spinning out of control.

The spotless white door of the ICU flung open and two doctors in white jackets walked out. Niloufer watched forlornly as they walked away quietly. Then a nurse emerged. She looked at Nishath. "The patient has stabilised for the time being. You may go in for a few minutes if you like."

Nishath turned to Niloufer. "You go in."

Her mother lay on a sterile bed. Niloufer gazed fondly at the limp form, tears pooling in her eyes. Multiple tubes connected her to various gadgets that blinked and beeped intermittently.

For a brief while she was alone with her mother.

But she didn't waste time. Quickly she opened the little box she held, took out the black amulet with strange brass beads and sliding up the sleeve of her mother's blue robe tied the amulet to her upper arm. And hurriedly she slid the sleeve back.

*

Hours crawled by…that tiptoed into days. She kept tab as it reached three.

Then destiny granted her a gift. Her mother showed signs of recovery. She sat up in bed the third day. She was hungry, she said, and ate her first morsel in several days.

A week later her mother was back home.

Was it the amulet? Did it even have any role to play? Or was it timely medical care or maybe just providence, she wondered.

But she didn't care.

A folio of feelings
by Anya Ramanujam

The Ending: CASTAWAYS

They both said their goodbyes
And
Turned away to leave.
They both
Had their backs
To each other
But they both wanted
To turn around and look
At each other.
Even if it was only going
To be as the last time
For them.
But
They held on
To their beliefs and ideas.
They wanted to run back towards

Each other.

They could have.

But

That is what

Held them back.

"So, is this what heaviness feels like?"

One of them

Thought.

"No..this is what letting go feels like."

The Other

Thought

Almost like a whispered reply.

Things would feel heavy

For now

But

It will soon settle down.

They were going away

To maybe come back to

Each other

Again

Someday

Or

Maybe

It was to be

Their last.

There could

Never be a

Conclusive answer

To this.

But

In this

Moment of

Separation

Even if it was

Physical

Somehow

They were

Still

Somewhere

Tethered to

Each other

Through thoughts.

The Middling: CHRYSALIS

When they both
Stood there
Under the neon yellow streetlight
Surrounded by the smoke rings
Made by now
Ashed out cigarettes
They didn't know
What to say
Or
How to say it.
Say anything
At all.
There was awkwardness
And
Sadness.
Maybe even disappointment
And
Possibly even
Regret.
"Never would have thought I would see you
Here."

It was

Neither

A question

Nor

A statement.

It was an

Empty

Hollow

Remark.

There was

Silence again.

The kinds that are

Uncomfortable

And

Unbearable.

A match was struck

Smoke rings conjured up

Again.

"Maybe life is truly…

Stranger than fiction."

It was getting colder

By the second,

Their breaths becoming

Condensed by the minute.
The yellow neon streetlight
Flickered a bit
The chilling winter haze
Was here to
Stay.
"I would have preferred fiction
If that was the case."

The Beginning: CATHARSIS

The last time
The ending
Was poignant
Enough.
The empty café was
A reminder
Of that.
A dazed summer had
Passed on for the
Winter haze
To come and

Settle down

Drumming against the

Wooden counter with

The cup of coffee,

Cappuccino

Which one had ordered

For the sake of ordering something

Had been left

Untouched and

Forgotten.

Anticipation and anxiety

Kept bubbling up

And

Falling flat

Again and again.

Was this right?

Was it too soon

Or

Was time still needed?

Wouldn't the ghost

Of the past

Haunt the
Living daylights
Of the present?
The ticking of the
Seconds hand on the
Clock
Above felt more like a
Blacksmith clanging on
A cast iron.
The noise would have become
Unbearable
At a point
Hadn't the doors of the café
Not suddenly opened up with
A loud ringing bell.
A gust of frenzied
Cold winter chill
Took over that
Small empty space.
With flurries of apologies
Coming in and the hurried
Rushing towards the ordering counter.

The clanging of the blacksmith
Faded
As the once empty stool across
Was taken.
A piping hot cup of
Black coffee
Sidled up next to the now
Stone cold cup of
Cappuccino.
"I'm sorry for reaching late.
I usually don't make this kind of
A blunder on a first date."
An eyebrow was raised.
"Did you intentionally try to
Make it all rhyme?"

As tentative looks were
Exchanged
As to what would be said
Next
A waiter arrived and brought
A fresh cup of coffee
Cappuccino

To the table.
Replacing the old with the new.
Now there were
Two piping hot cups of coffee
Misting up the windowsill
Against the wooden counter.
"If my intentions brought a
Slight smile, then I believe
Everything I just said
Made it all
Worthwhile."
The tugging of a slight smile
Did come
And for that moment
As brief as it would last
Everything seemed
Perfectly alright.

Talk of the dead

Have you heard the Whispering?
Across the Pond
Beneath the Cypress Tree
At 3:03 AM,
Is that the Time
You are Awake?
Awake...No,
It's more like being a Part
Of a waking Dream
A living Memory
But
With the shades of Unreal-ness
Becoming part of the Imaginary
Dreamtime.

Anyway

Have you heard the Whispering?
Beneath the Cypress Tree
Across the Pond?

At 3:03 AM?

Yes,

No…not Really,

I haven't slept for Years

To begin With

So to dream up Anything

Or

Walk past the black wrought iron Gates…

I stay within It

Under the sagging Willow Tree.

I have been There,

Shrouded under dark silk and Lace,

Faded now Obviously,

Since 1806,

So No

I have not Heard

The Whispering

Across the Pond

Beneath the Cypress Tree

At 3:03 AM.

Mnemonics of melancholic memories (repetition)

I

The witching hour
A lonesome tower
April showers
Jasmine flowers
Too young to die
Deep blue ink splattered skies
In the hour of need
Memories of my past bleed
I'm now just an empty shell
As you can tell
I'm putting you under a spell
Hear the tolling of the bell
It's now past the witching hour
The contents of the cauldron have now gone sour
There's an empty clearing
Where my end would be nearing
I'd like to say my last goodbye
Until the next time you find out
It has all been a lie

II

In loop

Repeat

Every word

Every meaning

Trying to find

Something

With them

Something

Unsaid

Something

Which was to come

But didn't

And the thing

That did come

Plain and in sight

For some reason

Just doesn't seem right

Or add up

Maybe

It'll take time

Maybe

It would need

Another rhyme
Another listen
Maybe
These are just…
Just thoughts
Fluttering in the air
Like the wings
Of a moth
Flying haphazardly
At night
Looking for a
Glowing ball of light
To end its
Brief
Existential
Flight

III

Stringing of thoughts
Turning in the locks
I bury my feelings
On the ground as I am kneeling

Hoping upon hopes
That things will end
I write it all down
But
Do not push send
Because what's the point of it all
But to keep on taking the fall
Each bruise and each cut
Brings a new lesson to be learnt
Silence and subtlety
Is key
And is understood by
Only you and me
Hush the voices
And
Dim the lights
Let's float our
Thoughts
Like paper kites
Travelling towards each other
Into these
Countless
Starless

And empty

Dark nights

Through these paper thin towns

With

Their flimsy papery lanes

While some would reach us

Safe and sound

Others would end up in the

Lost and Found

Who are you
by Chavi Jain

WHO ARE YOU?

Many of us have often come across such a question, but have we ever asked ourselves?

WHO AM I?

I am someone who'd feel like a child but is mature enough to make her own decisions.

I am someone who'd say exactly the opposite of what I want or what I feel.

I am someone who'd raise her voice wherever needed, but would take a silent step backwards whenever betrayed by my own friends.

I am someone who'd be scared from attachment, but would still get attached with all my heart.

I am someone who'd be crying all night and be completely miserable from inside but would still look perfectly fine.

I am someone who'd be there for anyone who'd need me but wouldn't be with myself when I need me the most.

I am someone who'd sit by the beach silently and would be calmed by the throbbing water.

I am someone who'd smile the things out which would hurt me the deepest.

I am someone who'd choose others' happiness over my own happiness.

I am someone who'd know the truth, but would still listen to your lies.

I am someone who'd find beauty in darkness and adore the moon for its flaws.

I am someone who'd talk to the flowers and watch them bloom.

I am someone who'd care a little more and worry a little less.

I am someone who'd want you so bad, but will still let you go, for your betterment.

I am someone who'd die holding hands with you but would never give up upon you.

I am someone who'd believe in miracles and would hope for them to come true.

I am someone who'd imagine the things out but would be too shy to make them happen.

I am someone who'd be strong as a rock in public, but would go through a breakdown all alone.

I am someone who wants to make her parents proud and would want to be an ideal daughter to them.

I am someone who'd actually make a difference instead of ranting things off.

All I've learnt through my teen years is that it's okay to just be you and not that perfectly woven girl because what's a moon without its flaws?

Just a light reflector.

Hence, it's okay to have flaws; you just need to embrace them.

All you need is to believe in yourself and focus towards the growth of your own self.

Eternity
by Devika Bajaj

Not in the mood to do anything,
Lying on my bed, just like this,
Watching my phone over and again,
Suddenly, I hear something.
Seems like a lion's roar,
I jump out of bed,
To see what's the thing!
And realize, not the tiger,
What steals my heart,
Is the roaring wind.

And then comes the rain,
That has the power to make me smile,
And dance while I remember,
I have a thousand reasons to cry.
Soon, I start to weep,
Because of this joy infinite,

The rain drops camouflage my tears,
And the laughter ignites.

I jump on the clogged water,
And it jumps back at me,
This feeling is so ethereal,
No, I can't describe the peace.
Cheers to the cheerful leaves,
It's their day to shine,
To live, as the wind blows,
A day for the hibiscus flower,
To brighten its color,
Into carmine.

I have no clue how it happens,
But my guitar strings,
Sound a bit sweeter,
When it rains in and out.
They carve out something new,
A flawless melody,
A symphony from beyond.

All I can say,

After the nature takes me away is,

Take me away,

Away,

From the hustle,

To the blooming bustle of the birds,

And the bees.

Take me out,

Out,

Of the noise,

To the peaceable noise of pacific tides,

And waves of the sea.

The Ice Cream
by Hemavathy Guha

It was one of those hot summer days in Delhi which those who have experienced it know very well how harsh it could be. The sun was shining mercilessly before it would hide behind one of those buildings after sun set. But the orange ball looked beautiful even in that scenario. Irrespective of the harsh weather conditions on that day, people were still going around on their routine jobs. Tired after a day's hard work, a woman walked towards the bus stand and waited for the bus which would take her home. As she waited for the bus in the shelter, her mind wandered and thought about the day's happenings, just like any other day. There was nothing special about it. She had completed her share of workload and handed it over. She squinted to see the number of the bus approaching. It was indeed the right bus. The yellow and blue colored bus came to a halt at the bus stand and she got into it.

The bus is less crowded, she thought. Yet the woman did not get a place to sit as there was no vacant seat. She was over 40 years old. When she was young and while travelling by bus, she used to offer the seat to anyone standing and who looked older. She specially felt for mothers with a baby in their arms. But these days, youngsters do not have any respect towards their elders and don't have those values. Or maybe she looked younger! The thought brought a wry smile to her lips. Well, it was just a matter of a few stops and she didn't mind standing. The DTC buses provided one of the cheapest and safest journeys in the city. Having found a corner to stand without being jostled by the others in the bus, she felt relieved.

She felt hungry and thought of buying something to eat when she got down at her stand. The thought made her happy. Before, she'd have very little money and would not indulge much in eating outside. During the winters, just a packet of hot peanuts kept her company till she walked the distance to her house.

The hot summer months and the humid monsoon days made things difficult for her. It rained very less these days. She felt hungry and thirsty too. An ice cream would just be the right thing to have today. She had some extra money to spend. Normally, when she took her children for outings, she got them ice-creams, but restrained herself from buying one for herself. After fulfilling her children's demands, she never had any surplus money left with her. Theirs was a middle-class family. After all, the ice cream is a luxury and not a necessity, she always consoled herself. She could do without it. Moreover, she might get a sore throat or might put on weight that would be more difficult to lose. But the motherly feeling in her made her spend on her children allowing them to enjoy.

Yes, it has been a long time since she had had an ice-cream. A rap cone would be delicious. Or maybe some new flavour! Her mouth watered. She thought of her school days and the endless number of ice creams that she and her sisters used to have while returning from school. How nice those days were! Her father also used to buy them ice creams whenever he had a chance. The ice cream those days cost only ten paise. She wished someone would take her to an ice-cream parlor and get her an ice cream. But no, she was a grown up lady. No one would think of that. She felt shy of eating the ice cream on the roadside all by herself. If there was someone to give her company, it would be good. But everyone had their own schedule of work. It's better to buy one now and enjoy it, she thought. Let people think whatever they like!

Her thoughts were suddenly interrupted as she sighted the bus stand. The bus halted and she alighted at her destination. Her eyes searched for the ice cream vendor. Sometimes, she has seen him on the other side of the road which made it difficult for her.

But today, the red and white box stationed on the same side attracted her. "Good, now I can have one and enjoy it," she said to herself.

She walked towards the vendor while searching in her handbag for the change. There was a hundred rupee note. There was no other change.

She hesitantly took out the note and asked the vendor, "I want to buy an ice cream. Do you have change for a hundred rupees?"

Not willing to let go of a customer, he mumbled something and asked her to choose the ice cream first. Her eyes went through the list as well as the accompanying price. A good one with an affordable price has to be chosen. She selected chocolate fudge and he handed it to her. He took the hundred rupee note from her and went around looking for someone who would give him a change. It was apparent that he didn't have change for that. This indicated to her that he had not sold much since morning. She had a feeling that he might not have been successful as there were not many people in the near vicinity. He first asked a man selling knick knacks squatting on the floor. No luck. He spotted a banana seller and asked him but, again, no luck. She could see that he would not be successful and called him back.

"Here, take back your ice-cream. I have not opened the wrapper," she said. "You will not be able to get it changed. I have to go home as my children are waiting."

She returned the ice cream, took back the money and placed it back in her handbag and started walking away. Maybe things would be in her favour some other day and time.

The Anklet On Her Left Foot
by Ipshita Mitra

"…she kept me warm in this unforgiving cold."

She opened her bleary eyes when the cat, all seven pounds of squirming flesh, climbed onto her belly. Squinting into the sunlight streaming in from the open window, she discovered that she was now the weary possessor of a pounding headache, and at some point, had managed to lose both a tooth and a spouse.

The words were ringing in her ears.

It'd been ten years that life had moved on for Sanjukta but the memory of that cruel winter weekend haunted her every season without any warning, or an apology. She woke up with a jerk. Her cat, after catching a few winks on her belly, had stealthily made its way into the kitchen. Summer months in Delhi were harrowing. Sanjukta was alone. The sky outside her window wore a hue that transported her to an unforgiving winter evening, a few forgotten years ago. Everything seemed to be at peace now. Everything was utter chaos then. Her thoughts meandered and she found herself drifting away…

~

Most Mondays, while driving to work, Sanjukta took a familiar turn, a curve that connected one of the dark alleys to the main road. This was her favourite stretch. School buses would crawl past and she would wave at the bobbing heads, trying desperately to peep from the window. Those smiles made Sanjukta's morning drive colourful and vibrant.

The lane across the pavement to her right opened to four little "neighbourhoods." She would slow down her car at each one of them. Four lives on the parallel road had become her extended family. A ritual. A routine. A tradition.

That day too, her foot hit the car brakes, and Sanjukta's gaze was fixed at these pockets that resembled four mushrooms popping out amid concrete and stones. Each mushroom opened up an umbrella of moments, some owed to routine, others unfolded surprises. Sanjukta soaked in these daily moments, daily. It was a story being written little by little, bit by bit, every day.

The florist stationed at one corner, a few metres from the gas station, watered his vivacious looking flowers. Not that it equaled a garden of exquisite plant life, but it was enough for a lover to pick a red rose that would, perhaps, later, wither away between the folds of his beloved's favourite romance novel.

Sanjukta was neither a lover, nor anyone's beloved. But flowers, she did love. Her husband, Nishit, would often bring her carnations. That was a long time ago. Nishit had vanished, only the fragrance of a bittersweet marriage lingered. Sanjukta had moved on but the flowers had, somehow, remained.

The florist switched between his blue chequered and white polka-dotted shirt every alternate day. The sole pair of distressed jeans, as the days went by, looked increasingly distressed, resigned to its fate, ready to breathe its last. Now that it was almost winter, he had pulled out a half-sleeved pyramid-patterned cardigan from his closet to keep him warm.

"Why do you have that frown drawn across your forehead, Ajit?" Sanjukta asked the blue-chequered florist, rolling down her car window that morning.

"Madam, my flowers are sick because of this pollution. Can't you see, they don't smile anymore," Ajit replied, morose, sparing a glance at the dying sunflower.

Before Sanjukta could dispense words of solace, the traffic light changed to green. It signalled her to move on.

She moved on. Like always.

Mornings were misty and evenings were foggy. Nothing was poetic about either. *Delhi is wrapped in a sheet of hazardous smoke*, TV reporters and radio jockeys announced. Even newspaper headlines screamed doomsday for Delhiites. People were choking to death. Masks and oxygen cans were up for sale. Oxygen cans!

Owing to routine, Sanjukta left early morning for work and returned late evening. Whenever she took the familiar turn to embark on her favourite stretch, she would find herself cutting through a film of dust and smoke. She slowed down at precisely four points during this morning exercise. She almost had the distance memorised, no, actually the number of speed-breakers.

At the third speed breaker, the stench of fish would reach her nostrils even before the humble space of Neel's fish market appeared. She could, as usual, spot the indigo blue lungi being flaunted by the rather petite fish-seller. Sanjukta thought Neel's round eyes had started to bear an uncanny resemblance with one of his robust Rohu fish. She would often think about it and laugh without anyone noticing her. Not even Neel's fish.

"Neel da, nice catch today, it seems. How goes the business?" Sanjukta would throw her customary question at Neel every Wednesday and Friday.

"All good, Sanjukta di, you must try my Hilsa. Delicious and at a great discount. Even your cat will like it very much," the fish-eyed Neel would chirp.

From between the parting of the tattered tent cloth, Sanjukta saw the anklet on Shibu's mother's left foot. The ends of her green chiffon saree moved like a gentle breeze. The bedsheet was the same as the day before, but her saree had changed, the anklet though was a permanent fixture. The second last stopover for Sanjukta was Shibu's tent. She adored the ten-year-old. He was smart, witty, and playful. And, his mother, a perennial sleeping beauty. Well, that's how Sanjukta had always seen her, at least in the last ten days or so. Before that, going by hearsay, she had gone to her village to be with her parents. Shibu was all by himself. What a brave boy, Sanjukta had thought.

Does she sleep all day, all evening, oblivious to the outside world zooming past? In her sleep, she must have traversed countless years. Or, was it that she was only up and about during afternoons, indulging her fatherless boy, tidying up her home, filling buckets of water, and cooking food on her dilapidated stove? All this, Sanjukta imagined while at work. She had never seen Shibu's mother awake. On her drive back home too, the scene would remain the same.

Who else did she have to call her own, who else did Shibu have to call his own? They were each other's owners.

The florist was missing that morning. The roses and the lilies awaited an address. Their fragrances were wearing thin, the smog overpowered like a looming shadow. Will the lovers and beloveds buy these exposed flowers that had already been tainted by the cruel weather? The drooping yellow lily had lost hope of sunshine, the sunflower had forgotten to look up in the sky, the morning was like a shroud of evening. The flowers were tense, how long could they go on like this: the cluster of red roses, crimson chrysanthemums, the dirtied white lilies, dahlias that detested dalliance with the coercive toxic winds seemed to be in a conference of sorts.

But where had the florist disappeared?

The last stop: Rishabh, the bangle-seller. He was busy counting the remaining glass bangles from his last stock of the red ones. 'Red is the colour of both anger and love. Isn't that peculiar, madam?' Rishabh had asked Sanjukta once. She was taken aback. Speechless, she went without any utterance.

Sanjukta's meetings with these neighbourhoods were closed on weekends. No office. No parallel reality.

Monday again, Sanjukta was late for work. She did not have time to stop by any of the neighbourhoods. In a hurry, she had missed a serious development. She had missed a tragedy, in fact. Or let's say, it came to her as postponed news. Shattering at that.

Sanjukta wanted to talk to Shibu that evening. Diwali sweets were pending. She wanted to surprise him and his mother. On her way back from the office, she stopped her car right next to Shibu's tent. She stepped inside, stealthily. The bedsheet was new. The mosquito net was rolled up in one corner. Everything looked all right, except one minor detail – the mother was missing. Sanjukta looked around, puzzled.

As if on cue, Shibu entered.

"Oh, Shibu, where were you? Look, I got you your favourite *Kaju Katlis*. Where is your mother?"

"I cremated her this afternoon. Been long pending."

Cremated. Pending. These words dropped like bombs. What did he even mean?

Sanjukta opened her mouth but no words would come out.

Shibu's tilted smile had shivers run down Sanjukta's spine.

"You know, I would often go to the gurdwara for the langar. I would leave early and return in the evening. That day, I didn't want to come back home to my dead mother. She had coughed blood the previous night and died without even letting me help her. She had been in cold shock." Shibu began the story of a mishap.

"It's been over a week since she died. After midnight, I started visiting the nearby cremation ground to steal burnt wood. The dead deserve dignity. At least, a shroud. My father abandoned us after I was born. He never returned to his wife and I never left his wife. She had coughed blood that night. But that was not unusual given that every winter, her lung condition would worsen. Eventually, she would recover. This time, she didn't." Shibu paused.

"But, why didn't you tell anyone? Did Neel know? What about Rishabh and Ajit?"

"Everyone knew. I would change her sarees every day, and wash her body twice. She had three chiffon sarees, anyway. Green, yellow and red. I didn't have enough wood to cremate her, di." Shibu's stoicism baffled Sanjukta.

"How could you survive like this for days on end, Shibu? Why didn't you tell me?" Sanjukta's voice was breaking.

"It was getting cold, di. It would get colder after midnight. A corpse doesn't move, neither does it change sides, nor snore. I'd fall asleep wrapping myself around her. She was my quilt. *She kept me warm in this unforgiving cold.*"

When she heard this, Sanjukta turned pale. A dead body as a shroud? The revelation stumped her. The twinkling stars in the sky dimmed and she felt dizzy and giddy with fear, helplessness, and shock.

Could this ever happen?

Shibu then led her to the corner behind the tent where he had been dumping stolen logs of burnt wood. Tears were stuck in her throat like a lump of dust and smoke. She was choking while Shibu went about recounting his story.

"I collected enough wood with Rishabh and Neel's help. It'd been a few days since I had been sucking all warmth from her lifeless body. It was time to return and repay, and give her the warmth she truly deserved. I know, I have been a selfish son. Now, tell me, do you think the pieces of wood that I gathered over the last week would have given her adequate warmth? But again, you didn't see the pyre, how would you guess?" Shibu asked, as he saw a frozen Sanjukta, her faraway glance now melting into and consumed by teary winks.

How could he be so matter-of-fact, dry, and yet so resolute?

This was heart-breaking and mind-numbing, all at the same time.

That evening, she drove, she drove mindlessly. The speed-breakers on her way made her car jump like a child on a trampoline. Each time, her car leapt, her heart galloped. Yes, she did have the road memorised, but that evening, everything had gone helter-skelter, the foot on the car's accelerator did not budge. With every jerk, her tears came gushing out, the blood in her veins curdled, the fireflies in the sky danced the dance of death in fury.

Sanjukta reached home, frazzled. Slumping on the bed, she thought about the anklet on Shibu's mother's left foot.

Wrapped in silken blankets, pillows, and satin sheets, Sanjukta was restless that night. She felt unbearably cold. Nothing helped. Nothing worked. She felt as if she was laying on a bed of dry thorns. Even in absolute darkness, her trembling fingers searched for the switch to turn off the lights. Every fiber in her body was shaking.

The cremation was over.

Should she go and ask Shibu how he was keeping himself warm tonight?

It's not always about living in the margins, it's about living on the edge too.

Tomorrow, she would ask the bangle-seller with a mole on his chin, "Is there a colour of helplessness too?"

~

Was it a dream or a nightmare? Everything was a blur.

Her head was throbbing. Nishit had hit her that night so hard that she lost a tooth. And then he disappeared. Did he really think Shibu was dearer to her? Shibu had lost a mother and Sanjukta a spouse. Both were victims, victims of doubt and helplessness.

Getting up, she stroked her cat, got ready and thought of stopping over at Neel's fish market.

Sanjukta and her cat had gotten used to the stench, after all.

- Poetry Collections by Parnil Yodha

The new shall replace us

We'll be gone, all of us!
Our stories shall lie 'bout
 untold, shattered on the
ground like pieces of what
used to be round bangles.

Our smiles, fits of laughter,
moments of tiny bliss,
years of suffering, bouts of
depression shall keep
echoing here unheard.

All of it shall become
meaningless: our efforts,
our pain, our survival…

All shall lurk within walls, and
the New shall replace us.

Severing me from me

Burns – swollen, red burns - across my chest, for
those narcissists stubbed cigarettes of ire on it.
Void numbness of emotional chock-a-block
 soaks my face, though embedded deep in my
unconscious are congealed blood clots that make
me growl if someone even pokes by mistake.

The tears I had not cried stayed inside me,
weighing me down with distrust and acrimony,
and settling down deep inside the bed of
a sea of seething anger, potent and
oppressive, which had swamped my mind like a
wave of tsunami, severing me from me.

Letting go

The leaf floats across the face of a sinister stream

of tugging thoughts that suck, push, pull and drag her down

to the black bottom. She resists, gives up, endures

and ploughs on, locking horns with the meanders of

the evil stream, guided by only flashes of

faint sunlight: brightness leaks, escapes occasionally through

the canopies of trees, and it dapples her with an

ephemeral solace 'midst consuming, dense black fog.

With the thought of a calm and tender memory – that

soars spirit, warms her soul – she weaves through darkness 'lone.

The mossy stones obstruct her path, but she swims and

persevere in the hope of a new sun-bathed dawn. And

she dodges the rocks of thoughts that remind her of
the moonless nights long gone, she doesn't want to
dwell on.

Those piano beats

Those piano beats resuscitate my beatless heart,
like water-drops stir a "dead" ant awake.
Fate lines on my palm are a puzzling art:
filigree of criss-crossing relationships.
Fairy lights glimmer on my body;
my mind, alas, is a New Moon sky!

Those piano beats pump out
the clogged pain from my parched eyes,
moistening my sclera;
nonetheless, my lashes remain a desert,
and chest a heavily loaded camel,
for thorns are my thoughts,
the mind's scoured enamel,
and the mood's steady as a sandstorm.

Those piano beats induce a mirage,

as majestic as an illusory oasis.

Hope, though, is a sand-coloured camouflage,

yet the depression is no longer as engulfing.

And they moved on, like nothing had happened

The beach:
her crushed body,
her smeared smile,
her kohl dark
memories in eyes.

Memories:
their transient footprints
across gray sand
and lasting secrets
stamped beneath land.

Footprints:
of all those who trampled

upon her, trundling and crushing
gravels, shells and pebbles
under their unfeeling feet.
Secrets:
swollen sores
in invisible pits
of her spiked skin
shovelled over with the sea.

The sea:
her hungry heart
overly clogged
soaking up
their self-centred sorrows.

At middle age

Suspended in mid-air
over a gorge, I dare
to put a foot on either Hill,
anxious as to where my sun is.

A child's slapped face,
on my right; nevertheless,
in her eyes, carefree-ness
lies, and resides resilience
of an elastic band.
Alas, unattainable!

Gums for a smile,
puncture wound for
a body, on my left.
Heart of a pilgrim,
beats to fend
off a painful end.

Alas, unavoidable!

Can't take it!

All the relationships shower like bits of
torn paper upon my demise. I'm trapped;
it's a dark well that keeps on getting, by
each minute, deeper; and its circular, black
wall's getting higher, closing on me like
pitch dark pits under eyes. Wring, wring my life
like sodden cloth, and watch the pain gush out!

Wedged in the door crack, I am; the door's
stuck. Helpless, I am squirming. Can't take it!

Clueless

Hope is scarce; I'm
breaking as the
New sun turns old
and sets, each day
on; a panic
comes, implodes and
undermines. Every time
I'm 'bout to make
it to the light
on the water
surface, something
or the other weighs
me down. Is it
possible that this
tunnel is a
circle with no
end? Am I just
wasting my time

by expecting more
rather accepting
my fate?

Nothing!

No feeling. No tears cried.
Nothing is inside. Void!
My insides have been clawed
into scraps and pieces
with razor sharp nails
of derision, disdain,
abandonment, gaslight,
rejection, blame and spite.

The strays are relishing
the flavour of the void.
Nauseous, I feel; my
abdomen hurts and my
oesophagus sears; my
head seems precarious like
an unfurling turban

under the weight of thoughts.

Death, death, I beg for death,
my only saviour.
A cobra is ahead,
ready to sweep 'n' swallow.
I am all braced up to
satiate snake's appetite:
cold meat for the snake.
Nothing else. Nothing!

Anjaane Rishte
by Monika Arora

Often sitting in seclusion, I wish that there was magic in my colors, which did not descend on the canvas. It enters people's lives in beautiful colors. No one lives alone in them. A fair happens with everyone, no one says that children are tormented, no one is worried about money, no one would ever feel hungry. If there was magic in my colors, how would I go through the world with my colors? I would end the game of pride and fill every heart with love. Love makes some new colors, I do everything that my heart wants, I wish that there was magic in my colours.

I could not, but yes, I tried to add color to many people's lives who met me in unknown paths and became very close to my heart. Perhaps so much that it is difficult to describe in words.

Fearing the wind coming from the afternoon or the sun, you have lurked on the branches of neem, walking in the corridor with brick floors in front of the red building. The lawyers have gone to their chambers, sitting in the canopy, somehow silent and obstinate questions in my mind. What should I do, my husband often says that a person of 27 is a little serious, why are you not now? I was angry. I was walking in the court campus with slippers, kept my belongings on the bench under the neem tree in front of the red building, a red leather purse, a steel bottle of water and an umbrella. I always kept my goggles on my head.

In the office meeting, I raised my hair and framed it, and I was making a plan. I was just watching my mangalsutra, and asked myself:

Is it really a symbol of love?

Coming out myself, I started looking towards the main gate, my eyes were searching for him. I saw a stranger was standing holding a file on the left side of me. He would be close to 40.

He sat down with me. My throat was cracking with thirst. Then I opened the lid of the bottle and reduced it to two sips of water. He was looking at my bottle very carefully. I asked immediately, "Would you like to drink water?" He smiled.

He said I saw you at the Trade Fair Delhi. I was a cool girl. No one's words have any effect on me. Again he started,

"Ma'am, you do your work very sincerely."

I was just watching him. I took off my mangalsutra and kept it in my purse. I asked him with a hiccup whether there was a hearing in his case today. He raised his head and said that the hearing would happen only when the case was made. "I come here like a madman, pray that she too Come but she does not come." What does it mean? After listening to his words, I started watching the soil, how dry the soil was. Relationships are also like land. When the soil dries out, love leaves its roots as if our love had left.

He asked me, "Do you work in Pragati Maidan?" I said no.

His stupid questions were disturbing me.

I was thinking of getting a divorce only. I too have started breaking the relationship between me and my heart. I am just wondering whether the little hands will be completely discharged now. What responsibilities would have changed even after separation?

Will life change after divorce?

I was thinking that soon the lawyer should come and prepare my papers and I will send the paper to Snehil and I will free myself from everything.

Will the lawyer be able to answer all the questions arising in my mind?

I don't know how many questions I was searching for answers for.

He gently shook me and asked, "Are you okay?"

I said, "Yes, I'm fine."

I said, "how can you get away from someone you love?"

He (the stranger) told me it doesn't work, we have to walk away from the one we love.

Maybe love grows by staying away.

It didn't take time to fall in love so much we don't care, we leave the one whom we once loved.

Right now I have just come to talk to the lawyer because I have taken a little time looking here and there.

He (the stranger) said that it does not take as much time to fall in love as it takes to leave. How much I loved her.

While listening to him, a word stuck to my ears, "love." And the past pulled me towards myself.

Seven years ago, when I and Snehil met each other. The family of Snehil came to our house to see me for the first time and I was sent to the balcony to talk alone. My family was sitting here in the drawing room and were talking. Snehil was looking at me and he told me how beautiful I was. "Just like an angel!"

After talking about jobs etc., I was completely silent but my mind was not.

"Do You want to ask me something?"

"Is there something special about you? So tell me about yourself."

I said, "Yes, I am not fond of cooking at all."

"I love to roam, I am a little temperamental. The family says that love has spoiled me but I think I have a basic nature." I looked at Snehil and said while keeping a cup of tea on the stool.

He said, "I want to love your basic nature."

He took my hand in his hand.

His touching…touched me deep inside.

Believing my every insistence brought him closer to me.

Will I get some water, this voice of his has brought me out of the past

I was completely empty.

I was watching the newly wed couples walk down the corridor.

How the two were looking at each other, how much love was there.

Both were looking at each other as if what they have they got today.

I asked myself, if there was so much love between both of us, then how did so many fights come?

A voice came as if someone was singing a song, tum hi toh meri dost ho…

He (the stranger) said, "I hum sometimes."

He (Snehil) never had time for me, he would never wish me a birthday.

Sometimes the hand was shaken and sometimes it was broken without talking.

Sometimes his head would be broken.

Sometimes I took him to the doctor.

Was it anger, love or madness? I don't understand.

He says later, "Sorry." And I behave the same way again.

I forget all.

Now slowly starting again, as I had become used to all this, I was just a toy for him when he felt like he would play and then remove it.

He probably never liked my praise, only my shortcomings could be seen from him.

Again the same voice fell to me from the corner of the past.

Then the same voice dragged me from the corner of the past and brought me to the present.

When some drops fell on my head, he (the stranger) said that the rain is coming, I'll get wet.

"Come, let's go there." I smiled. He was watching me, and he said, "Your smile is very sweet."

Snehil also used to say things like this.

I started asking myself again, Snehil, why have you changed so much?

Seven years ago, the past stuck in the chest, then started pulling me back like a magnet.

I was seeing that stranger again and again. Why is he talking to me with so much interest? Then I took out my diary and started turning the pages of the diary.

Those pages of the past dragged me back into the past.

Seven years ago, some new changes were taking place in my body. I came to know that I am going to be a mother.

I was not ready for all this but Snehil's age forced me, and after three years of marriage our family was complete with a lovely daughter, and then after 2 years, a son.

But soon I realized maybe the family was not complete. The burden of responsibilities had come at the age of 23. Now he did not want anything from me.

Then again the same voice came. "Will you pray for me? She must come here today and sign the divorce papers and set me free. Will you pray for me?" He was repeatedly saying to me with folded hands. I was watching him.

Is divorce really so relaxing?

He started coughing.

I took out the bottle and gave him water to drink.

I asked him. "Are you fine?" He said, "Are you fine?"

I went and stood beside him.

I replied, "How can a person standing on the threshold of divorce be?"

"Will you tell me?"

"Why do you want to take it?" he asked.

I came back and sat on the bench.

"There's nothing left between us like before, so I want to get divorced."

He said, "Nothing ever remains the same as before."

"There was a very strong love between me and my wife too, tightening both the palms of their limits," he told me.

Slowly he opened his palms.

Some cops were going to handcuff a man.

Some people were coming back separately with divorce papers.

I again asked him, "Is it wrong or right to get a divorce?"

He said that it is not right to take divorce in a hurry. Then he kept quiet for a while, then he said, "I did not make haste. I had told only with great love for one day that I want to divorce you. Then she went to her maternal home, since then I am waiting for her to come and divorce me."

Then a very sweet voice came. "Papa!" In front of us a 17-year-old girl was standing, who was wearing jeans and a shirt. With curly hair she looked very cute.

"Papa, you are here again."

I said, "He is waiting for your mom."

She looked at me with a full eye and then while sitting in the empty space between us. She said, "I know he is waiting for my mother."

He also knows she'll never come."

I asked why?

She said, "Mother never wanted to be separated from him. That's why she left Papa and went away forever."

Then she looked up at the sky and started crying loudly.

I hugged her and loved her so much.

I started feeling the pain that those who leave never come back in life. Our three pairs of eyes were looking at the sky.

All three of us had become statues.

Ma used to love Papa very much and Papa was always angry.

Mother always used to say that your father loves me very much but he does not know how to express it.

One day, my father got angry and said that I want to divorce you, she could not bear this word and started going out with me in anger.

Papa snatched me from her lap and she was going alone to Nani's house when she met with a truck accident on the way and she ended up on the spot.

Father could not forget mother's departure and till today he thinks that he threw her out of the house and she will come back.

Whenever father forgets to take his medicine, he comes and sits here and waits for my mother.

He still doesn't realize that she has left us forever.

My Mother rightly used to say your father loves me so much.

Then she asked me, "Aunty, are you sitting here for a while? Till then I will bring an auto for Papa."

"Yes." I nodded my head.

She ran out as soon as she heard my voice.

I went to that stranger and said, "you should not take divorce from your wife. She loves you very much."

He said, "Yes, I will not give her. I have come to take her back. Just once she comes here, I will say that I will never be angry with you now. Please do not leave me, divorce is not right. Which divorce are you taking?"

I said, "I don't know which one I am getting. I don't know whether I am getting divorced or not."

He said to me again, "Don't tell him that you want to get a divorce. He will leave you and won't come back again."

Like I sit till today waiting on this bench that she doesn't come to me.

Similarly you will also keep waiting and he will not come.

Because those who leave don't come back.

The relationship of husband and wife is like a hot one,

Without which every taste of life is incomplete.

Sometimes the salt of the gums,

Sometimes the sweetness of happiness,

Sometimes the bitterness of the fight,

Sometimes so sweet to celebrate each other,

Sometimes tasteless silence,

Sometimes tadka talks,

Life is incomplete without this taste.

Expectations are made in love,

full of compromises, under compulsion.

Do it, love is not right,

It keeps indifference

That's enough

For a person

Who wants to get into someone special's heart.

It is not that he understands No,

Just reads more of the world,

Then every moment is cut according to it.

Keep your account clean from life

Everyone wants you, like you,

Keep it unaccounted,

If there is some torch in love,

It will go far,

Wet memories will not be able to stop it.

So you too go home and don't get divorced.

I started crying holding his hand

You are right

I'm going back home.

My kids are waiting.

He (the stranger) gave me his number and said, "Ab tum hi toh meri dost ho. Kabhi kabhi call kar lena." I gave him my number.

By then his auto arrived.

 And I took him slowly to the gate.

Tears were flowing from my eyes and I was thinking again and again whether one word can change a person's life like this.

I had come to the court to get the divorce paper prepared, but I didn't know what I was carrying today. Maybe today I got the one I was waiting for so many years.

It was the feeling that changed my whole life.

How easily we break up.

Today I was realizing that whatever will happen will happen, now I will not get a divorce.

How my life is
by Aman Aryan

LOVE. INSPIRE. FREAK. And ENJOY.
Mingled with every fragment of the journey we start.

Having that warmth
That feeling of being cared
Cuddles all along and the moments we shared
Slumbers in the day and
those long winters with bae
Dreaming together for together we stay.

The sun went away, now again the time's to sleep together
Again the love will bloom all the way
As this season passes into another.

Stroking her hair, caressing her lips
Beholding her smile...my every hour flips

Hearing my name...on every word of hers
Reading myself...in the eyes of hers
How couldn't I care more for her
By finding myself in every answer of hers.

Framing those conscious hurdles
For together we were, it seemed special
Even solving the solved puzzles where
Every clue connected us.
Where every equation was made to solve us.

How beautifully my mind frames such things for me
Where I live in illusions and that girl lives in me.
 Hallucinating the sweet love of ours
I tried to paint the first wall.
Now you strike off LOVE from my life
Because now I know that wall's too tall.

With pride and valour I claimed My ship sailed to a new harbour.
Leaving LOVE behind, INSPIRE as named.
Ideal is the way I preach,
Truth is the fact I share,

Glory is the fame I have,
And pleasure is what I feel.
I feel the crowd crying for me.
I hear the people praying to me.
To myself… I am less than a star.
I am the one whom I admire the most,
I am Lucifer Morningstar.

Hell NO, someone cries inside me.
My hallucinations have not stopped yet.
The hell high I am right now.
Right now I'm no more inside me.

I nixed the second wall of the thing.
Now this one is more of my type I guess,
One freaks to have that taste for once,
I FREAK out for my whole life is a mess.

I flip this leaf from the book of my life.
I take it as a good sign.
ENJOY is the new tag I can see
To which all humans must align.

Two souls at my back always,
Always I have those desires I wish.
I vibe and sing the Bella ciao,
I am the New Professor now.

Party, Vibe, Sing, Dance and what all one can add.
You throw a new verb for me,
I'll build a new passion of my own.
I am the man of power and possession,
I am no Adam who dies alone.

I am having my ball I think,
I think I have something after all,
Or it's the pills playing ping-pong again,
Again it's the pink elephants standing tall in the hall.

No gadget can give me what all I wish,
No marvel can bring the light of hope,
No magic can cast a spell of happiness,
No meds can bring me out of this..

There was no tooth fairy for me,
There is no Santa in all the winters,

No wish I made was heard at all.

Life was dull to me,

Still bright for all.

No love, no charisma, no joy brought a way to me,

I had a door to sneak and freak out, I told you... I am the Lucifer Morningstar

And the new room was hell to me.

Jumbled up mysteries, no wings to fly

And acceptance is too far to guess. And interestingly… this devil is LOST and left to die.

I'm IGNORED... oh yeah… the hell I am...

Why not... I'm F**KED after all.

Kurt hasn't been admired ever before..

"Nobody dies a virgin. At the end life f**ks us all."

This journey wasn't meant for a journal as such,

I think I might take a rest for forever,

I think I'll leave this room alone,

I think... I'm EXHAUSTED so much.

LOST. IGNORED. F**KED and EXHAUSTED.

Mingled with every fragment of journey I had… The journey I had to tell.

I had no Chloe on this earth.

Maybe I have none in my hell.

The Black Pawn
by Naviya Yaduvanshi

Azalea Selene was seven years old when she was first introduced to the Black Academy. That was the first time when she was told that she wasn't ordinary. Nine years later, she's a student of the Academy. It isn't a normal academy. The Black Academy is meant for special children, not ones with genius brains or who are differently abled. Children in the Black Academy are far from normal, they are extraordinary— they possess supernatural powers.

The Black Academy is supposed to be a shelter for the supernatural kids, this had been told and advertised to the supernatural community. But behind the perfect mask, the Black Academy made killers. The students of the Black Academy are trained to be assassins, the best of the best. Their powers are moulded and shaped to fit the needs of a world-class assassin. But not everyone can become an assassin. The students of the Academy must be vetted before they can be sent into the field. For that, the selection was devised. A six-stage competition through which all students from the age of sixteen are put through. The weak are killed and the strong advance. At the end of the selection, the ones left standing are the ones that become The Black Academy Assassin.

Other than the maiming and killing, the Academy wasn't all that bad. Azalea had made a few friends who she cherished, Elizabeth, Anna, and Ben. They had their own problems, their own fears, but somehow, they just worked. They are all sixteen, meant to go through the Selection, and become Black Academy Assassins. It wasn't going to be an easy task, she knew it. But, with her fears, even knowing that gave her no advantage. She doesn't fear the killing, instead she loses herself in it. That's what she fears. She fears loving the feel of the kill, she fears killing her friends. The Selection isn't a place where there are unicorns and rainbows, it's a bloodbath. From the first stage of the Selection, the rules are changed, maiming another student during class is allowed and encouraged. Killing moves during a spar in a class is allowed. But, that's not all, Azalea discovers something behind the scenes. An interesting character and her plan. She finds out about the White Queen and her Black Pawn. The White Queen's plans are vague, but it's clear that her plans encircle the main character of her story, the Pawn. And Azalea Selene is a candidate for the position of the Pawn. Throughout the Selection, she finds more about the White Queen's plans. The White Queen wants to destroy the company. The Altera Company is meant to be stomped and crushed under the Queen's feet. And the Queen intends for the pawn to do so for her. At the last stage, after suffering through something only a few people have experienced, Azalea finds out the last piece of the puzzle that she's been decoding since the first stage. The White Queen's identity! The Queen is none other than Victoria Casella, the headmistress of the Black Academy. And her Pawn is Azalea Selene.

About the Authors

Akber Ayub

Trained to be a mechanical engineer, sailed the seas for over a decade in the merchant navy, then did a stint with the five-star Taj group of hotels as a project engineer. Later, set up couple of industries in Bangalore exporting to Europe. Was a college faculty for some time and finally heeding an inner call turned a writer. Started with freelancing full-time on travel for mainstream newspapers, inflight and other niche magazines and doing assignments for corporate in-house publications in between writing newspaper editorials. Contributor to niche spiritual magazines and others, like a Times Group publication. Later, worked on coffee table travel books on southern Indian states of Kerala and Karnataka as writer and editor. Author of the book Marine Diesel Engines and contributor to one of Jack Canfield's 'Chicken soup for the soul' series of books. Author of a suspense thriller set in Kerala.

Anya Ramanujam

Anya Ramanujam is currently a freelancing content writer based in the capital city of New Delhi. When she isn't jotting down poetry and stories you'd see her either devouring a mammoth sized book or vehemently debating over some film or series she has recently watched. She's old school at heart but also ever so curious to venture and experience the new.

Chavi Jain

Chavi Jain lives in Delhi. She is a student of Rajdhani College, University of Delhi. She loves to express herself with the help of different mediums like poetry, music, art, calligraphy, dance and many more. She is trying to explore herself in different fields of work and is willing to make a career in the world that interests her the most.

Devika Bajaj

Devika is a writing enthusiast. Every word in every stanza of every poem, she believes, has a meaning so intense that one cannot understand, but feel the essence of it. Her poem "Gratitude" was published in a recent anthology, *Morning Mist*. She's looking forward to all the opportunities that might help her dissolve into the world of writing.

Hemavathy Guha

Hemavathy Guha is a well known visual artist and writer. She has been writing on art, architecture and travelogues for the past 15-17 years in leading magazines like *India Perspectives*, *Discover India*, *Swagat*, *The Eclectic*, *Creative Mind* and *Rashtriya Sahara*. Of late she has also been contributing to digital platforms like artsome.co, matterofart.in. Her essay on "Tracing the Trajectory of Illustrations in Tamil Periodicals" was recently selected for the 'Write/art/connect' grant by Serendipity Arts foundation 2021. This is her first submission for a short story competition.

Ipshita Mitra

With over 10 years' experience in publishing and journalism, Ipshita Mitra has a Bachelor's degree in English Literature from Miranda House, DU, and holds a PG Diploma in English Journalism from IIMC. She did her MA in Gender and Development Studies and is currently pursuing her PhD in Gender Studies from IGNOU. She has worked with *The Times of India, The Asian Age, The Quint*, Om Books International, World Monuments Fund India Association, and The Energy and Resources Institute (TERI). In 2016, her short story "Cacophony of Silence" was published by Nikkei Voice, a Canadian-Japanese newspaper. In 2020, her short story "Bohemian Sailor of the Gulf" was published by Sublunary Editions, a Seattle-based independent publisher. *The Indian Quarterly* (April–June 2021) published her short fiction, *Kabuliwala Returns*. She writes on books, culture, environment, and gender for *Feminism in India, TerraGreen, The Hindu, Scroll.in, The Wire, Wasafiri, Firstpost, Huffington Post, India Currents*, and others.

Connect with her on

Twitter: https://twitter.com/ipshita77
Facebook: https://www.facebook.com/ipshita.mitra.1/
Instagram: https://www.instagram.com/ipshi777/

Parnil Yodha

Parnil Yodha is a writer-poet based in New Delhi, India. Her works have been published in literary magazines like *Borderless Journal,* FemAsia, *Indian Periodical, Indus Women Writing* and *Setu Bilingual.*

Monika Arora

Monika Arora is an eminent artist and writer. She is a painter and an artist with a difference. She is an inspiring story of a self-taught artist and a businesswoman who tries to do best in all fields. Now she decided to follow her passion for art and writing and wants to dedicate her life to it. A story of rise to success in a short span of two and half years with dedication, devotion, proper planning and understanding of business, marketing and many other fields. She is also a teacher, a writer and a poetess.

Her works have a mysterious quality... a magical touch that makes them stand apart from the works of other people. Everything that she paints or writes has a deep meaning and message in it. May it be a single sentence, story or even a canvas. Her works are many a times a transformation from realistic to abstract.

She deals in rainbow colour palettes and her paintings reflect fantasies and dreams.

Aman Aryan

Aman Aryan is a student of B.A. (Hons.) English at Shivaji College, University of Delhi. He is a writer, poet, standup performer, and a proud literary enthusiast. He has co-authored many anthologies. He is also the brand ambassador of an internationally acclaimed organisation i.e. Protect Your Mom.

Connect with him on Instagram @aman__1905 or write to him at *amanaryan1905@gmail.com*.

Naviya Yaduvanshi

Naviya Yaduvanshi is a high school student, born in Lucknow and brought up in various cities across India and UAE. She has been an avid reader since a very young age which influenced her to create her own stories and characters with their own adventures. She was inspired by various authors who put words to their thoughts in the form of a book. This led to the birth of Azalea Selene, and her first novel, *The Black Pawn*. The synopsis in this anthology serves as a teaser for her book. In addition to reading and writing, she also loves art and music. They are the two other passions she cherishes the most. Last but not the least, she also loves to hang out with my friends.

www.ingramcontent.com/pod-product-compliance
Lightning Source LLC
LaVergne TN
LVHW041535070526
838199LV00046B/1684